TRUE FEELINGS OF THE HEART

ANURAG A. SEGEKAR

Made with ♥ on the Notion Press Platform
www.notionpress.com

Dedicated to my Aai (Sau. Namowanti A. Segekar)

and Baba (Shri Arun Segekar).

Contents

Preface

For me, love is the feeling of trust that you get when you find someone trustworthy. Not someone you completely give your life to, but rather someone who makes you want to live it. I believe you develop a strong feeling that the person is right for you rather than falling in love. Love is something that binds everyone while also breaking that same trust. Everyone has an opinion about love; whether it is a blessing or a curse, we don't know. But one thing is certain: even the most isolated person on the planet will go to any length to find the right one.

In this story, you will see the ups and down occur in the romance of two people, how they overcome it to enjoy the togetherness.

Disclaimer

This is a work of fiction. Any names or characters, businesses or places, events or incidents, are fictitious. Any resemblance to actual persons, living or dead, or actual events is purely coincidental.

CHAPTER ONE

GOING TO SCHOOL

"Wake up, Alissa," my mother said from downstairs in a motherly tone she thought was empowering. Me on the other hand thought it was just plain sweet. I yelled back in a low tone, "5 minutes please," and then fell asleep again, only to be woken up by my older brother Damon pouring a bucket of water on top of me, causing me to burst in rage. "WHAT ON EARTH IS YOUR PROBLEM?" I screamed so loudly that I broke the glass on the nightstand next to me. "I just wanted to jolt you awake. I warned you before I did it, so don't freak out. Today is our first day of school, so hurry up and get ready. Be down in 25 minutes or you're walking to school." I nodded, and he walked out the door, closing it behind him.

I stood up and went to my closet. It was a massive structure with red doors and black handles. I went through my entire closet before deciding what to wear today. I chose a strapless blue and white top that flowed down to my waist, black skinny jeans, and white gladiators with silver diamonds at the top. I put my clothes on the bed and went to my bathroom. Yes, you read that correctly. MY restroom. This was a wealthy family. My father was a doctor at the largest hospital in town, and my mother was a designer who designed dresses for most of the hottest singers out there, including Selena, Nicky, and others. They both made a lot of money, and as their child, I got a portion of it as well.

I went into the bathroom and locked the door. I forgot to lock the door the last time. Damon and his friends Liam, Zayn, and Justin came in and took my bra and taped it to the front bulletin board for all of the students to see. It was extremely humiliating.

I turned on the warm shower and waited a few seconds before entering. I shut the door when I got in. I stood there for 5 minutes, allowing the tiny drops to trickle down my body and into the drain. It relieved my achy muscles. I then took the soap and rubbed it over my skin. I reinserted it into the holder and washed the soap traces away.

I then took the shampoo and squeezed just enough out. I massaged my scalp with the liquid until it became foamy. Then I rinsed my hair and turned off the water. I grabbed two of my soft white towels as soon as I stepped outside. I wrapped one around my body and another around my head. I entered my room and went to my drawers to get my underwear. It was a black cotton bra with silver lines running from the top to the back, and the underwear was the same. I grabbed my jeans and pulled them up to my waist after slipping them on. Then I slid my strapless shirt over my head.

I walked to my little table in the corner and placed all of my girly items on it, such as my straightening iron, make-up, and other girly items. I plugged in my curling iron and set it down on the table to heat up. It was taking too long, so I grabbed my make-up bag and pulled out the essentials: eyeshadow and lip gloss. I rubbed the light blue eye shadow onto my eye with my finger, making sure it was light. Then I smeared my lip gloss onto my perfect lips. I didn't need much make-up because I was already beautiful. I had diamond blue eyes with a silver tinge to them.

I began working on my hair after I finished applying make-up to my face. My hair was night black and stopped up to my boobs. I curled each piece of hair to my liking. Not too curly or fat. Just \sright. When I was finished, I stood up and walked over to my body length mirror. I took a look at myself and liked what I saw. Back in school, this would have shocked the guys who picked on me and the girls who called me fat. Smiling, I ran downstairs, grabbing my gladiator and back pack as well as my cellphone.

My mother was preparing her breakfast in the kitchen, while Damon was already seated at the table with his friends. Damon and I had a similar appearance, except he had chocolate brown hair and hazelnut eyes, he was 6'2 while I was 5'6, and he was a year older than me.

Liam, who was 6'1 and had black hair like mine, was really good at sports, had a 6 pack, and was a total hottie, sat at the table. He was very popular with the girls, and I had a secret crush on him. Zayn sat beside him. Zayn, like Liam, was 5'11, had brown hair with one black streak, and was yet another hottie, but he already had a girlfriend named Katy. They were engaged at the time, and she attended the same school as him. Justin was the last person to sit. He was fine; he had blood red hair that looked brown in the sun and ruby red eyes with a hint of silver. He also had four packs.

We all rushed outside to Damon's car after I finished eating. I called the shotgun. The boys were vying for it, but I got there first, forcing all three of them to sit in the back. It was a 15-minute drive. While we were driving, the guys all made small remarks about how I looked. "You look smokin' hot today, Alissa, but that's no surprise because you're always hot." Liam stated. I flushed and turned my face away from the window so he couldn't see. "Thank you; you look great today!" I said it casually, but inside I was screaming.

When we arrived at school, all the boys were looking at us with lust in their eyes. I smiled at them and waved. Then I noticed all the girls staring at my brother and his friends. They were all extremely popular among the local ladies. I said my goodbyes and promised to see them at lunch, then entered the school. I entered the school one step at a time. As soon as I entered, every memory flooded back to me. The positive ones involved me and my real friends, and the negative ones involved me being bullied and called names. When I thought of it, I felt a single tear start to fall down my face. I quickly whipped it away and reminded myself that I was no longer the ugly girl who was constantly picked on. Now, I felt strong, self-assured, and most importantly, BEAUTIFUL.

I inhaled deeply before flashing a broad smile in place of my frown. I still have a good memory of this school. Even though I already knew where everything was, I did notice a few changes since my last visit three years prior. To get my schedule, I strolled over to the office. I had to ascend three flights of wooden stairs because it was all the way upstairs, then I had to pass through a small hallway. I walked into the office after arriving there and opening the door. Though she appeared different, the secretary was the same. Her name, if I recall correctly, was Mrs. Seith. She was once 4'5" tall and had blonde hair cut short. She now appeared to be around 5‘6 tall, had black hair that reached her shoulders, and could pass for a teenager. She was hiding her face in a stack of paper when I walked in and didn't notice me. I successfully attracted her attention by clearing my throat.

She gave me a shocked look as she looked up at me. She gave me a hug the next thing I knew. "I also gave her a hug back. Oh my goodness, you must be the returning student Alissa. You've changed a lot! I've missed you so much, so I'm glad you're back!" She almost screamed. I exclaimed, "Hey Mrs. Seith. Yes, that's correct; I‘m back, and I also missed you. She at long last relinquished me, and a tad. We talked about some new happenings around the school and my life before I left. She instructed me to sit while she looked for my schedule after we were finished. I simply got up and took a good look around the office for a few minutes. Everything had changed. The entire office had leather chairs and wood tables, and the walls had been painted a light blue. To tell you the truth, it appeared to be better than before.

I sat in a black chair against the wall because it was taking her longer than I had anticipated. Now I had closed my eyes. I relaxed them for a few seconds because they hurt. When I opened them, I saw Mason sitting next to me and recognized him. I didn't like him, and I utterly detested his thighs! I have an excellent explanation, so you might think I'm being mean right now. However, that must wait. He simply smiled as he looked at me. When I asked, "What do you want?" I made an effort to be as polite as I could. but it came across as a tone of annoyance. I just wanted to meet the new student and see if I could ask her out. I looked at him with complete resentment. I'm sorry, but I already have a crush on someone, and you'll get to know me better as the school year goes on." After I mentioned that, Mrs. Seith resumed my schedule. She gave it to me before turning to speak with Mason.

After ten minutes, Mrs. Seith had requested that Mason show me around the school, but I said it was fine because I still remembered where everything was. However, fuckin' Mason consented to it, and he was now escorting me around. He took my calendar and read it. You and I both take the same classes. So just stick with me until you know where all of your classes are." I put all of my books away and grabbed the ones I would require for the morning as he walked me to my locked door after he said that. When math class started, I went to the front of the room and said hello. All of the guys were just staring at me and drooling before I said anything. I grinned and said "Hello everybody, my names Alissa. Some of you may recall me being bullied in middle school, while others may not. I just wanted to let you all know that payback is a snob. I could see the shock on everyone's faces now. Thanks." I smirked at Mason as I looked at him before returning to my seat. After that, I moved to the back and sat next to Tyler, a hot-looking man.

The math teacher, Mr. Sean, just gave me an encouraging glance. He then started teaching the lesson for today, and even though I knew everything, I paid attention to everything. As well, I took notes. I left Mason behind as soon as the bell rang, signaling that our next class was about to begin. I walked all the way to study hall, sat down on a chair, started listening to my music, and started drawing in my notepad.

CHAPTER TWO

What the Hell?

I was taking in; When someone suddenly took my headphones out and threw my notepad across the room, I was listening to Want You Back by Cher Lloyd. The lights went out and I heard the doors close. Ugh. When some moist, smooth lips crashed onto mine, I was surprised and looked back to see who was responsible. It was too dark to see, so I didn't know who it was at first. I quickly pulled back and stepped back.

"Who on earth are you?" I pressed. They continued to get closer to me without saying a word. I found that I kept moving away until I was face-to-face with the wall and had nowhere to go. That individual was presently before me. They refused to move when I attempted to push them away. Instead, they pinned my arms around my head and grabbed my arms. I tried to scream and protest, but their lips were still on mine when I opened my mouth.

The person whose lips these are was an excellent kisser. In their embrace, I felt like I was melting. I felt like I was kissing a silk bow because their lips were so silky. I noticed that they were asking for entrance when I noticed something wet slide across my bottom lip. I didn't say anything for a few seconds before I felt him bite my lower lip. He took advantage of that and slid his tongue into my mouth as I gasped. I had the impression that I was just paper; both fragile and weak due to his careful tongue movement; investigating my mouth. After pulling back to get some fresh air, the lights came on. I was absolutely shocked by what was in front of me. Mason was it. I allowed him to kiss me just then. While I fell to the ground, he smiled as if he had just won the lottery. Will you go out with me, Alissa?" Holding on to the walls for support, I lifted myself up from the ground. I looked at him from above and said, "You gotta be kidding me. I FUCKIN HATE YOU!" After that, I left and went to get my belongings.

It was finally time for lunch. I was all flushed as I left study hall and made my way to my locker. You couldn't believe who was standing there when I got to my locker. Mason was the one. UGH, what are you looking for now? "That was all I said. Okay, I know what I did to you in the past makes you think badly of me, but I've changed. I could demonstrate it to you if given the opportunity. Just one chance, please." I only said, "OK, just leave now," before he left. I stuffed my books in after opening my locker. I waited at my locker until I saw a brunette I recognized, along with three others I recognized.

"Hey, you guys miss me?" I asked as I approached them. When they saw me, their eyes lit up with excitement as they all turned around. "Alissa?" Before giving me a huge group hug, that was all they said. When I last visited three years ago, all of them were my closest friends.

They treated me well and were actually my friends.

"Yes, I am. The singular Alissa Martine" I flashed my flawlessly white teeth with a bid smile. You look absolutely stunning!" The brunette said. Emily was actually her name. The blonde boy said only "Oh My God." Alex was him. The other two just

taken a gander at me dumbfounded then said "Hold up, you looking hot child

gurl!" It came from Lissa and Stefan.

"You all look incredible as well." Following my statement, we proceeded to the lunch room and formed a lunch line. I grabbed an apple juice and a slice of pizza. Then they paid at the cash register all the way. We sat at the table in the middle of the lunch room after Emily, Alex, Stefan, and Lissa paid for their meals. We talked for a long time. After that, Liam came up behind me and gave me a cheeky kiss. I rounded the corner and drew him closer to me. I then got up and gave him a hug.

We walked to our bags, grabbed our water bottles, and we drank all of the liquid that was left in them. I prevailed in a one-on-one basketball match after we were done. The era had come to an end, and it was time for art. This time flew by quickly. Art was my favorite subject because it allowed me to express myself in a variety of ways, like; coloring pages, for instance. I went to my locker after it was finished and saw Liam waiting for me there. I rushed to him and gave him a cheek kiss. We then walked to his vehicle. A shiny red Jeep was there. You have no idea how much I adored it. Like a true gentleman, he led me to the passenger side and opened the door for me. I boarded the driver's seat while he took the passenger seat, and then he dashed off to the movie theater.

CHAPTER THREE

Movie Theater

Mason was staring at us before we left to go to the movie theater. He was looking at Liam as though he were some garbage. I could tell from the way he looked at me that he was about to cry.

I turned to look away because I didn't want to deal with it right now. After that, Liam rushes to the movie theater.

"Then, who were you with during the fourth period?" inquired Liam

I pondered his question as I looked at him. Uh, not really anyone." I responded with. "Um, really?" Okay, just a boy by the name of Mason. He was merely asking me questions. Now Liam was quiet. He said nothing bad. I decided to turn the radio on because it was so quiet. I sang along when *Call Me by Carly Rae Jepson* started playing.

I threw a wish in the well
Don't ask me, I'll never tell
I looked to you as it fell
And now you're in my way
I trade my soul for a wish
Pennies and dimes for a kiss
I wasn't looking for this
But now you're in my way
Your stare was holdin'
Ripped jeans, skin was showin'
Hot night, wind was blowin'
Where you think you're going, baby?
Hey, I just met you, and this is crazy

But here's my number, so call me, maybe
It's hard to look right at you, baby
But here's my number, so call me, maybe
Hey, I just met you, and this is crazy
But here's my number, so call me, maybe
And all the other boys try to chase me
But here's my number, so call me, maybe...

When we arrived at the movie theater, I suddenly stopped singing. I simply sat back in my seat and turned off the radio. "You're a good singer Alissa," Liam said while he was looking at me. I expressed my gratitude with a smile. After that, we exited the vehicle and met the guys and their partners.

It appeared that not everyone was sitting together. We were watching the movie together at the time. The movie theater was divided into various sections for each couple. Zayn and Katy were in the front, Justin and his girlfriend Celine were in the side, Tyler and Veronica were on the other side, and my brother Damon and his girlfriend Elena were in the middle. Liam and I were in the back. Zayn and Katy were in the front.

I could already see Justin and Tyler having sex with their girlfriends before the movie started. Damon had just placed his hand on Elena's shoulder as she sat next to him in a cosy position. Only Liam and I really weren't doing anything. Then, just when I least expected it, Liam joined their fingers. He gave me a grin as I looked at him. Next thing I realized he pulled me on top of him and caused me to sit on his lap. Thank goodness it was dark so he couldn't see my face because I blushed. He put some of my hair behind my ear and removed some of it from my face. Then he whispered, "Alissa," into my ear in that sexy voice. I turned to face him, and their lips met. I wanted more after he gave me a soft but passionate kiss. I began playing with his hair as I snagged my arms around his neck. He hand his arm folded over my midriff. He graciously granted my request for entrance after I bit his bottom lip. His lips met mine as my tongue slipped into his.

Together, they danced to a ba-ba-bam beat. He groaned as I lightly pulled his hair back. I kissed his lips with a smile. After that, he did something odd. I was pushed back onto my seat after he pulled back. He didn't look at me for the rest of the movie, and when it came time for him to take me home, he didn't say a word. Now I was so angry. That is, you kiss me and then ignore me.
Why is that the case?

I pulled the handle to open the door when we finally returned to my driveway. Before I attempted to open the door, all I heard was a click. He shut it off. "Open the damn door before I break it," I said after taking a deep breath. He spoke after remaining silent. Only if you say you'll forget everything that happened at the movie theater." I was stunned. He was requesting that I disregard everything.
Now, my blood was boiling. You know, I was wrong to think that you were different. Just what the rumors say about you.

Consider everything that was overlooked. I used my key to open the front door as I walked in. I ran to the bathroom after slamming the door shut in my room. I need to take a shower to forget about what happened. I couldn't stop crying while in the shower. My heart just broke for the person I used to love and admire.
My tears weren't apparent on the grounds that it was mixed in by the water. After heaving a sigh, I began washing my body. After that, I left ten minutes later. I pulled out a bra and pantyhose when I went to my draws. Purple was the hue. After putting them on, I put on my pajamas. They were made up of a; blue tank top with white shorts.

I got into bed and pulled the covers up to my neck after I finished dressing. A few minutes later, I drifted off into a deep sleep.

CHAPTER FOUR

Overlooking With A Sprinkle Of Envy

Beep, beep, beep, beep, beep. Ugh that dumb morning timer just wont shut the fuck up. I was still a portion of a rest when I attempted to stir things up around town button in any case, my hand slipped and hit the hard floor. "Owww" I shouted then got up, immediately holding my hand ensuring it wasn't broken. I looked at the morning timer with contempt composed all around my face then, at that point, took it also, tossed it across the room. It hit the stopping point and broke into about 250 little pieces. Extraordinary I thought. Presently I really want to purchase another one on my way home from school. I was as yet not feeling better because of what had occurred on the earlier night with Liam. I recently concluded that it was ideal to continue on also, disregard him. Strolling over to my wardrobe, I opened the entryways and chosen my outfit for now. It was a green little skirt with a red sleek bow in the center and a red tank top. I laid my outfit on the bed what's more, strolled to the restroom. At the point when I peeled my garments off I picked them up and place them in the hamper. Then I strolled to the stand-up shower and turned the tap to cool.

At the point when it was amazing I strolled in and shut the entryway behind me. Iremained against the wall allowing the water to run down my body then, at that point, down to the channel. Briefly I could of swore I heard somebody open the entryway to my room, get it was only my creative mind cause I saw no one. At the point when I was back in the shower I snatched my watermelon scented cleanser and scoured it onto my body. Then I took the matching cleanser and kneaded my scalp. I washed off and came
out 2 minutes after the fact. I got my skin dry and slipped my garments on. Then, at that point, I strolled over to my little table and chosen to simply fix my hair. I stopped my fixing iron in and hanging tight for it to warm up. At the point when it was done I part my hair into various areas and started to deal with it. 18
minutes then I was finished. Next was make-up. Gee green eye shadow with some unmistakable lip gleam I thought would look great. I took it out of the make-up pack and sliced some eye shadow on, then scoured some lip shine on my smooth lips.

Presently all I needed to do was have breakfast and I could hustle and get this day over with. I strolled first floor just to track down Liam and Damon finding a spot at the table. What extraordinary karma I have. I went to the refrigerator and taken out a container of squeezed orange and swallowed it done. Ahhh that was invigorating. After I said farewell to mother and strolled to the front entryway. I could hear strides behind me and I could as of now think about who they had a place with. "Alissa stand by. I really want to converse with you about an evening or two ago" I didn't make eye to eye connection with him. I recently said "Sorry uhm do I know you, and what are you discussing?" Then I left. Outside pausing for me was Mason. He had needed to converse with me for some time now so he messaged me today, and I let him know that he could get me and we could talk about it on are method for tutoring.

At the point when I left I saw Liam gazing at me. He looked beat red. I didn't actually however, care. Basically I wasn't the person who was being a jerk. I bounced into the traveler side and locked in. Then, at that point, Mason pulled out of the carport and continued advancing toward school.

"Sooo what you want to discuss?"

"I simply needed to express heartbroken about everything. I realize I have been mean to you for the several days, and I was contemplating whether I still had that a single opportunity left to demonstrate it to you."

"Alright, could you demonstrate it to me today?"

"Suree, today after school would you say you are free? I need to take you out some place extraordinary."

"Definitely, I'm. Sounds great. I'll hang tight for you by the storage spaces then later

school."

"Alright, I guarantee I wont be late." We were at long last at school, and Mason stopped right close to Liam. Damn it. I got out and saw Liam resting on his vehicle gazing at me. I turned away, and simply keeps conversing with Mason. At the point when I passed him, he snatched my hand and pulled me back. "Relinquish me please" I said not thinking for even a second to look at him without flinching. He wouldn't give up, so I pulled my hand away from him in a fast development and proceeded strolling to the storage spaces. At the point when I arrived, Mason had previously left me. I opened my storage also, stuffed my books in. Then I snatched the ones I would require today. It was a brief time frame plan meaning we just had 3 periods in the morning today then we could leave. My periods for now were Workmanship, Recenter, and Science. I got my books then, at that point, shut my locked and continued to my top of the line workmanship. At the point when I was most of the way there, somebody snatched me from behind and held a material to my face. I planned to shout and drive them away however I didn't have a lot energy.

Next thing I realized my vision was getting foggy, and everything I could see presently was dark. I felt myself drop to the floor. Then somebody got me wedding style and conveyed me some place. At the point when I awakened I understood that I was attached to a seat. What in the world was going on? I attempted to

move my options however they were limited tight. I checked out the room that I was being held in and remembered it. It seemed as though Liam's room however painted an alternate shade. "Hi?" I called out ... be that as it may, no answer. The entryways out of nowhere flew open and I saw Liam strolling in. I shouted
what's more, said "Liam unfasten me right now or i'll kick you where it really hurts hard at the point when I leave." He chuckled and said "No, Yet you can attempt." I raised my leg to kick him, yet I neglected to do as such. UGHH!
(Liam's POV)
I was down the stairs while Alissa was higher up. I was making her something to eat, seeing that when she awakened she would be hungry because of the impact of the medication. I would have rather not harmed her, however she wouldn't pay attention to me. Rather she disregarded me. This was my last choice. I saw her strolling to her most memorable period class, and nobody was near. I made a move to catch her, and get her out of here before anybody took note. I adored her, and I expected to tell her that. At the point when we were at the cinema I kissed her. It was the best kiss I at any point had in my entire whole life. Her lips were so delicate like a holy messengers from paradise. I needed more. However at that point it hit me.

This was my dearest companions sister. What in blazes would i say i was doing? I rapidly removed her from me and pushed her back in her seat. All through the entire film, I did whatever it takes not to check her out. It was so difficult reason she was right close to me and she continued to gaze at me. I manged some way or another. At the point when I dropped her home, I got some information about everything. She looked beaten down and said I was very much like what the tales said about me and that everything was neglected.
I felt horrible. I was unable to rest that evening. The sum total of my thoughts was Alissa and how I treated her. She should detest me at the present time. I went to her home the following morning and she kept on disregarding me. I was in a real sense pissed at this

point. That is where this plan came in. I had as of now worked it out with Damon, and he let me know that it was cool. He took note that I had profound affections for Alissa and he felt that I was keeping down as a result of him. He said that he wouldn't see any problems assuming I dated his sister, yet on the off chance that I at any point hurt her he would remove my child producer. The fact that he was OK fulfills me with it. It makes this a ton simpler. Presently all I needed to do was account for myself to Alissa and trust that she pardons me.

"OK you have five minutes to pick up the pace and account for yourself previously I begin overlooking you always." That was all I told Liam. I was distraught.

Who in the fuckin damnation would grab somebody and afterward drag them to their home? Well obviously Liam would. Hes reason should be worth my time. I need to meet Mason in almost no time and here I was caught in Liam's room restricted. Decent eh?

"Alissa simply kindly listen to me."

"Unfasten me first!"

"No, assuming I do you will run."

"I wont run I guarantee. Simply loosen me please."

"Alright fine."

Liam at long last unfastened me and when he was going to speak, I set out toward the entryway. I ran, while he pursued me around the house. A couple of something else steps and I would be gone. At the point when my hand was on the entryway, Liam snatched me and turned me around. He pushed me facing the entryway then, at that point, crashed his lips onto mine. Good gracious! His lips were warm and feel so delicate. I wound up answering. I wound my arms up to his neck and played with his hair, while he wound his arms around my midsection holding me. Both of are eyes were shut. This kiss felt so unique like it was implied only for me. Lips are formed together in amazing shape like they were made for one another.

Liam bit my base lip and I joyfully separated my mouth for him. He slid his tongue into my mouth gradually and started to investigate my mouth. I pulled on his hair delicately and he groaned.

Next thing I knew we were on a rough surface. My conjecture was a bed, yet how did we arrive? Liam kept on kissing me, he turned us over so he was presently on top of me. We pulled separated for air. I just gazed into his chocolate earthy colored eyes, while he gazed into mine. Right away I grinned. He grinned as well and showed his ideal silvery white teeth. Then, at that point, he kissed me once more, yet this time it was a delicate yet enthusiastic kiss. He pulled back and started to trail kissed down my neck. At the point when he got to my collar bone he sucked on it. I was groaning, and I had no control over it. It felt much better. Before he could do anything more I turned us over so presently I was the one on top.

I sucked on his neck and gave him a hickey. I grinned like I won a award. Then I did likewise he did to me. Sending kissed down his neck and afterward sucking on his collar bone. He groaned while I just chuckled. I got off of him and set down close to him. "So what are we presently?" I asked out of relax. "Were sweetheart and sweetheart," said Liam in a sure tone. Goodness truly? I thought. "Alright assuming were sweetheart furthermore, beau then I have 1 condition." I said. "Alright name em." Liam said. "I would rather not be a mystery couple and I maintain that we should carry on like beau and sweetheart." I said a bit
humiliated. "OK darling." I kissed him again yet this time it was a minimal longer then a moment. I pulled separated when my telephone rang.

"Hi?"

"Alissa? Its Mason. Is are date still on?"

"Goodness ... howdy Mason. Sorry i must drop."

"Why?"

"Cause I have a beau now. His names Liam." When I said that I taken a gander at Liam and grinned.

"What on earth?"

"OK well byee." I said and hanged up.

"Who was that?" asked Liam. "Just Mason. we were assume to go out on the town today, however I as of now have a beau so designs got dropped and I surmise hes frantic now yet anyway." Liam looked pissed. "What? You were the person who advised me to fail to remember everything so I concluded the time had come to continue on, however at that point the following day you hijacked me and made me fall head over hells for you once more." Presently Liam was grinning like a doof.

"Alright time slipping away, so might you at any point drop me home?" I inquired.

"OK" was all he said. We strolled back ground floor and out the front entryway to the vehicle. I got in the traveler side while he got in the driver side. It was a 10 minutes drive to my home. At the point when Liam pulled up in the drive way, he got out, and came around the side and opened the entryway for me. I got out and snatched his hand lacing are fingers. At the point when we strolled in Damon was Elena were in the family room along with the folks looking discouraged. I strolled in and asked what occurred. Then, at that point, everybody went to me and they began shouting in entertainment. "Gracious MY Horrendous Damnation Both of you ARE DATING?" asked the folks. I just gestured my head and pulled Liam nearer to me until are lips were contacting. I kissed him and afterward turned around to face them.

"No fair. Why Liam gets the cutie?" Shouted Justin. I in a real sense fell down giggling. "Since I love him. That is the way he got me." I addressed that inquiry. Then, at that point, I saw Liam's face light up like a child at the point when they first see sweets. "Whats up with you?" I inquired. "You just said you adored me!" I become flushed and gestured. He snatched me and turned me around. "I love you too Alissa Martine." I grinned then he put me down. I expressed night to the folks, and went up to my space to go rest. Liam recently followed and I let him.

CHAPTER FIVE

TRUTH OR DARE

Me and Liam were both in my room. He was resting over this evening. I was wearing a white tank top with dark shorts to rest. Liam then again had stripped out of his garments just leaving on his fighters. He got into bed with me, and pulled me closer. I rested my head in his chest and fell a rest a couple of moments later. "Get your butt up Alissa and Liam, were playing truth or dare night adaptation." shout Damon from first floor. I covered my head with the pad attempting to shut out all the sound. However, it didn't help because two seconds after the fact every one of the folks; Justin and Tyler were up in my room hauling both me and Liam ground floor.

The entryway ringer rang a couple of moments later. I had welcomed a portion of my young lady companions because I realized they would be available. At the entryway stood; Emily my best bud, and Rachel one of my dear companions. We as a whole embraced, then, at that point, I pulled them in. Everybody sat all around. "OK i'll go first." said Tyler. "Truth or dare Rachel?" Rachel in a real sense was grinning a major ass grin. "Dare" she picked. "I challenge you to strip furthermore, kiss three irregular folks in the city." Rachel grin transformed into a grin. She striped her garments leaving on only her bra and underwear. She strolled outside and we followed. Strolling as an afterthought walk were 2 adorable folks. She approached them and gave them both a kiss on the lips. Then, at that point, there was an elderly person seeming to be around 45 years old. Her sneered dropped to a nauseated face. She approached

him and
however, kissed him.

When she returned she took a gander at me and said "Truth or Dare?" My grin out of nowhere dropped. I abhorred her insights or dares, and moronically I didn't think she planned to ask me. "Uhm .. . Dare" I answered. "I challenge you to have a one on one make out meeting with Liam right here this moment." I saw her like she was at last crazy yet got up also, moved to Liam at any rate. I plunked down confronting him then I pulled him closer until are lips were contacting. This was a hot kiss. It left me needing more. I crashed my lips onto his and gave him an energetic kiss. It was long and sweet.

He chomped my lower lip till I allowed him access. At the point when I did he slipped his tongue into my mouth and investigated it voraciously. He maneuvered me onto his lap with out breaking the kiss. Then he pulled back and began to leave a path of kissed done my neck the whole way to my collar bone. He halted and sucked it. I was groaning like insane when at last the folks pulled him away from me.

I was a radiant red at this point. I took a gander at Justin and Tyler and said the well known three words "Truth or Dare?" The two of them picked dare and I said I dare you both to french kiss everybody here. They looked disturbed yet did it. At the point when they kissed the young ladies they didn't need to break a section. It resembled 2 magnets stuck together. I pulled them a section and said OK you folks are great. In any case, they got me furthermore, nailed me down. The two of them kissed a side on my cheek then, at that point, let go. "Ewwww now I have an entire pack of spit on my cheek." I rushed to the restroom and washed it off.

At the point when I returned Emily was responding to an inquiry. "Emily is it valid that you love Tyler" Justin inquired. Emily was presently red as a tomato. She turned her head and gestured. Then Tyler's eyes illuminated. I as of now realized those two enjoyed one another however they were both to terrified to just own it. However, tyler chose to take the main action. He got up

and strolled to her. He pulled her up then nearer to him, and kissed her delicately on the lips. She wound her arms up to his neck and played with his hair. While he got her midsection and pulled her significantly closer. She licked his base lip and he conceded her entrance ensuring not to squander a second. He slid his tongue in to her mouth while she did
the equivalent. Then, at that point, they pulled a section to get their relax. They just grinned at one another. Then, at that point, Tyler accomplished something so charming. He said "Emily will you be my sweetheart?" Emily illuminated like a shinning star and said "OMFG YES!" she embraced him and they refreshed their relationship status on facebook. Presently the entire world realized those two were together.

Everybody left a couple of moments later, while I approached my room and set down on the bed. Liam was right next to me. He held me in a warm hug. Ensuring that I was staying put. I turned around and embraced him and said "Goodnight child, Love you." He grinned and said "Lovee you more." Then I headed back and
begun to count sheep ..... 1 sheep, 2 sheep, 3 sheep. When I got to the forward one Liam took out his blackberry and gave it to me. I took a gander at it and saw that he had changed his relationship status. It presently said "In a relationship with Alissa Martine" I was so cheerful presently, that I got up and kissed him on the lips. Then I fell a rest a couple minutes after the fact.

CHAPTER SIX

PLEASURED

I wasn't actually sleeping. I was unable to. I could hear Damon and Elena moaning in the room next to mine. Liam decided that it would be okay if we went to his house while I slept the entire night. I foolishly wore a white tank top and black skinny jeans and left the house right away.

When we got to Liam's house, we went upstairs to his bedroom. He walked over and pulled a white long t-shirt out of his drawers. He threw it at me while indicating the restroom. I walked over to it and closed the door. I then started removing my clothing. I put on the white t-shirt once I was done stripping. Liam's scent was all over it. I loved his smell. It wasn't musty and gross like the smell of all the teenage boys. It smelled strongly of lemon. Which I prefer.

I gathered my clothing and folded it into a tidy pile. I then noticed that Liam had already changed into his clothes when I opened the door. His boxing shorts were blue. He was just lying on the bed, but he was so dashing it made me drool. He didn't have a shirt on. It was easy to see his six pack. I joked, "You can now stop drooling over me."

He walked over to me and I sped away. I dashed back into the bathroom and closed the door behind me. I overheard him say, "When I catch you, I'm going to do wonders to that body of yours." I was blushing, so I exited the bathroom through the other door. Liam was following me closely. I hurried back to the bathroom after going back to the bedroom. Exactly a few steps away. Before I could turn the knob, a large arm encircled my waist and forced me onto the bed. After standing up, I wrapped Liam's neck in my arms and pulled him close to me so that our lips were barely an inch apart. I pushed the space between our lips together and kissed him on the lips as his arm rewound around my waist. He moved his body closer to mine, trying to close the gap between us.

As our bodies came closer and closer to one another, we were unable to move because of the pressure.

Without letting up on the kiss, I turned us over and rode him. As I retreated, I began kissing him on the neck. As I stopped, I sucked on his collarbone. He moaned, and I started to listen. I stopped and moved in the direction of almost nothing Liam after sliding my hand across his rock-hard abs. Liam was growing taller by the day. Before I did anything else, Liam told me, "Alissa, don't do it," as I removed his boxers. I'm going to get you back if you watch." At any rate, I smiled however did it. We got into sexual intercourse. Liam said, "Alissa, I adore you. I kissed him and grinned before adding, "I love you too." He pulled back, and we both landed on the bed.

"That was awesome!," I exclaimed out of breath. Alissa, I know how much I love you. Liam spoke softly. While he wrapped his arm around my waist, I just smiled and cuddled up next to him. Then, at that point, we both nodded off into every others arms a couple of moments later.

CHAPTER SEVEN

SECRETS

I entered the classroom and settled in. Liam hadn't arrived yet; at school and that steamed me in light of the fact that for the beyond couple of days he hasn't called me back, instant messages, or even messages! He really worries me a lot. What if something bad happened, or perhaps he no longer likes me?

I stopped because my brain was hurting from thinking about this. A couple of moments later Mr. When Fitz arrived, he began his lesson. However, there were two reasons why I was not paying attention: I already knew this, and my mind kept thinking back to Liam. I stood up and walked out the door to the parking lot when the bell rang, indicating that it was time for our next class.

I didn't care that I was being followed because I had to see Liam right away or I would die. I proceeded to walk all the way over to my vehicle and extracted my bag's keys. Someone grabbed me as I was about to open the door and turned me around. Mason was it. That's what I thought: Oh no!

"What do you need Mason?" I asked attempting to pick up the pace.

" Where do you suppose to go?" He instead inquired. Nothing to do with you!" I almost yelled. He was burning through my time and I was in a real sense passing on. He then backed me up against the car after taking my keys and throwing them in the grass. I don't care that you're not going anywhere. Take notice of what Liam is doing to you. If you were my girlfriend, don't you think it would be better? I would respond to all of your texts, emails, and phone calls."

"Stay quiet. How would you realize something terrible didn't occur?" He looked at me as though he was debating whether or not to tell me something. Simply let it out!" I yelled. "Nothing bad happened... I know that because were brothers," he said after a brief pause. We were concerned about what you would think, so we didn't tell you," Mason said quietly.

I was now laughing so hard that I was on the ground. Haha, you're so funny, I doubt I'll believe you without evidence. He picked up his phone and dialed Liam's house number. Mason replied, "Mom, its Mason I was wondering what time do we have that family thing at." His mother answered and said, "Hello." I'm coming right after school because I forgot. "Hey dear, it's tonight at 7:40PM," the women on the other line said. However, Liam will arrive a little late. Ensure you dress pleasantly and bring a date." She then ended the call.

I was practically frozen in place. Am I deaf or did I just hear her correctly? My goodness! As I fell to the ground, Mason held me up. "Okay so anyways the reason why Liam's not here is really unexplainable," he said to me while I was still inside his car. Instead of hearing, I think it would be best if you saw." "Uh, okay," I said as I just stared at him. Will you be my only date tonight?" I hesitated before responding "Yes" when he asked.

"Okay, we'll cut class early because we need to properly dress before we meet them," I was perplexed. Isn't what I was wearing sufficient? He got the car moving and started it up as he left the parking lot. To get to our destination, we had to drive for fifteen minutes. I got out of the car when it came to a stop and saw that we were at one of the best dress stores in this area.

Mason reached out his hand and walked over to my side. I didn't back down because I was still a little weak. He picked out a nice blue dress and some heels for me as we entered the store. The dress didn't have any straps and was 2 inches above my knee. It was blue, and the top had heart-shaped bead patterns. The belt then wrapped tightly around my waist and hugged my body. The remainder of the dress simply fell down. The dress was very distinctive yet elegant.

Another story concerned the heels. I cherished them. Diamonds were atop them, and they were black. About 5 inches off the ground was the heel. They seemed strong and beautiful. There was a slight clacking sound on the floor with each step I took. You appear to be breath-taking. Mason said, which made me blush. Thanks." I offered a calm response. We made our payment by walking over to the cashier after I finished getting dressed. He paid, despite my insistence that I should, but he wouldn't let me. "I'm the one who forced you to come along so I will," was all he said. Due to the fact that it was designer brand, the total came to $200. After we had paid, we got back in the car and drove for an additional ten minutes.

In front of a nice store, we stopped. Given how well the name represented boys, I assumed it was intended for all boys. We strolled in and Mason let me know that I could choose his outfit. I grinned and went around the store till I tracked down the ideal outfit for him. It was made up of: a white dress shirt, black skinny jeans, a classy silver watch, a black tie, and converse shoes to complement the entire ensemble. When he emerged from it, he observed my drooling. " It's funny, Alissa is drooling over me. I wiped my mouth with my hand after he said that just to be safe. Heh, no drooling. Nuh-uh." That was all I said before we paid at the cash register. The sum was roughly $175. When we were finished with all that, we strolled back to the vehicle and Mason started driving once more. I swear this was the longest drive I've ever taken. We have been driving for the past hour while confined to the vehicle.

Mason got out and walked around to my side when the car finally came to a stop. I exited when he did the same for me. After closing it, he extended his arm. I clutched it while he lead me into the extravagant looking eatery. The interior was painted a light pink. The wall was covered in numerous pictures of various things. The tables were arranged in various positions to give off a very romantic yet peaceful appearance, and the floor was made of flawless white tiles.

The waitress showed us to a table when she arrived. I was amazed when we got to the table. I tried to flee, but I was unable to. One side of the table held Liam, who was surrounded by a girl like glue. She had short black hair and light brown eyes. Liam's eyes widened in surprise when he saw me. Mason sat next to me as I took a seat. Mrs. and Mr. Matthew were seated side by side at the table. This was downright off-kilter. The silence was broken by Mrs. Matthew. So, Amy, you and my son have been out together for how many months? That was probably the name of the girl who was sitting next to Liam. Mrs. Matthew, we only started dating about two weeks ago. She responded by acting completely innocent.

Mrs. Matthew gave me a look of disgust when I looked at her. However, I already knew why. Amy was disliked by her. Amy appeared more like a slut than a girl. I was furious because she was so attached to Liam. However, I decided not to cause a scene here. Hello, dear, Mrs. Matthew turned to face me. That outfit makes you look absolutely gorgeous. I assume you and Mason, my son, are in a relationship? I saw her amazement and before I could say anything Mason talked rather he said "OK mother, were dating." Following that, Mason did something unexpected. He gave me a kiss on the lips. I didn't say anything at first, but then I did. After giving him a kiss back as gently as I could, I stopped breathing. "Yes, we are," I replied with a smile to her. He is the love of my life. Mason heard Mrs. Matthew smile and whisper, "She's a keeper." Already, I adore her." I smiled and didn't say a word.

We ate and talked as the waiter arrived and took our order a few minutes later. Mrs. Matthew got to know me much better. She even insisted that I call her Seara, which was her first name. Seara, her husband Paul, Amy, and Mason left after we finished eating. I promised to text Mason tonight, I told him. Liam and I were now on our own. Given that he had cheated on me with a slut, I didn't really want to talk to him.

I mean, at least do it with a real person if you're going to cheat on me! Not a slut at all! Were finished." was all I said before getting up and going away. Liam had not attempted to explain himself, and he was certainly not following me. I let a tear roll down my cheek before wiping it away and going outside. Mason was waiting for me outside.

He rushed up to me and gave me a hug. While he held me, I cried incessantly.

He then drove me home and inquired about staying the night. Even though I wasn't thinking clearly, I said he could. He turned off the engine when we got to my house and walked with me up to my door. I entered after opening it. Due to the fact that everyone was already asleep, we walked slowly up to my room. I went to my dresser and pulled out some sleeping gear. After that, I went to the bathroom to change. I was now donning a t-shirt and shorts. When I came out of the bathroom, Mason was already lying on my bed in his boxers. My goodness!

He was provocative. I'm aware that I shouldn't be thinking this, but I just can't help myself. He had a 6 pack. After putting him in bed with me, I turned off the lights. He encircled me with his arm, and I did not move. He drew me in until we were so close that it was hard for me to breathe. I turned to face him now that I was on my opposite side. Let's make a wager, Alissa." Mason stated I wouldn't back down because he knew I loved betting. Okay, you're up. What exactly is the bet about? I inquired. I have one week to make you fall in love with me. I promise to stop and give up on you if I lose. You must agree to date me if I win. I felt a little downhearted and like my heart was getting smaller when he said he would give up on me. I have no idea why.

"Okay, good." I smiled, turned around, and a few minutes later, I fell asleep in Mason's embrace.

CHAPTER EIGHT

THE BET

The Day Three:

I accepted Mason and myself's wager. Mason had behaved like a gentleman throughout the entire week. That was odd because he rarely displayed this side of himself. He was always with me in the morning, at lunch, and when he drove me home, he sat next to me in my locker. Over the past two days, he has not once attempted to touch me. However, today we are going on a date after school. I don't know if we were going to the movie theater then.

After Class:

When the bell finally rang, it meant that the hell hole could be left for the day. Mason was sexily leaning against the lockers as I was walking to my locker. He chose me despite having all the girls falling for him. He made me feel special in some way. I adored the outfit he was sporting today. It was made up of: He then wore a pair of black skinny jeans, a lime green t-shirt, converse, a silver watch, and a chain that was low on his jeans. He had the hot bad boy look because his hair was messy. I thought it made him look cute. I gave him a quick hug when I got to my locker and then put my books away. Mason lightly grabbed my hand after I was finished and twisted my fingers together. I hid my face, blushing a little, to keep him from seeing what he was doing to me. We walked to his vehicle, where I boarded the passenger seat and he boarded the driver's seat. We arrived at the movie theater shortly after pulling out of the parking lot.

Movie Theater:

We arrived at the movie theater after a ten-minute drive. Mason followed me out the door first. He came over to my side and once more took my hand. I was becoming increasingly anxious. I sincerely don't have the foggiest idea why. Like it was about to break, my heart was pounding hard against my rib cage. Uh, strange feeling? Was Mason harming me in any way? We continued walking together all the way to the line. We had to wait ten minutes to get our tickets because there was a long line.

I let Mason pick the movie when we were at the front. He asked for two tickets to the movie "Couples First Love." The movie was romantic and funny at the same time. We sat in the middle row when we entered the theater. Because you had the best view, that row was known as the best place to sit in a movie theater. Throughout the movie, you could see couples already having an affair, while others just sat there looking into each other's eyes or doing things like; snuggling, holding hands, etc. I sensed that someone was looking at me. My side of the face was being punctured by the flames. I veered off to look at Mason. His eyes were filled with lust for me. I simply smiled and returned to the monitor. The movie was pretty good. I just saw half of it however since my brain had pondered back to Mason. After the movie was over, we left the theater and walked back to his car. While he was in the driver's seat, I was once more in the passenger seat. He got in the car and drove to his house all the way. I apologize for forgetting to inform you that I am staying there due to family issues.

Upstairs:

I sat on Mason's bed after walking all the way up to his room. Mason appeared after a few minutes. He was surprised to see me on his bed, as I typically slept in my room. He approached me and cradled my face. He got closer until their lips finally met. He gave me a tender kiss. I responded quickly and without delay. I gave him a passionate kiss back. He then tried to bring us closer together by bringing me closer. We were currently on the bed. He was kissing me from above. After taking a breather, he began to kiss my neck.

I groaned in delight. While I assisted him in removing his own, he took off my shirt. We were in bed naked a few minutes later. This thought made me blush. Mason gave me a neck kiss before coming to a stop at my boobs. Before sucking on them, he stopped there and used his tongue to caress them. I was happy yelling his name all you could hear. M-M-Mason!" I screamed numerous times.

After that, he came to a stop and pushed his finger into my core. Two more came after. He was turning them around and twisting them. I shed a few more tears of joy. After that, he slowly took them out, which made me very wet. I exchanged positions so presently I was on top. I imitated him. After giving him a few kisses on the neck, I sucked on his collar bone. I became interested when he moaned. I went down until I reached Little Mason. You could see that Little Mason was getting taller by the second, so he was happy. I sucked on Mason's dick while smiling. Thank goodness, it wasn't that big. I added more to my mouthful. Now, at least three-quarters of it was in my mouth. Now, Mason was groaning incessantly. He may not have been able to control it. Lissa sucked a lot harder." Mason stated But I did it. He held my head and directed me. Gently he pushed it up a bit making me take in all things. Shortly thereafter, I retreated. I was surprised by something Mason did. He started shoving me with his dick. Several back and forths. It hurt at first, but once the pain subsided, it was okay. He remained in me, and I then felt him cuum. He sucked my boobs once more after rubbing the tips of his fingers against them. I yelled out his name. Then we both collapsed on the bed as we pulled back. I simply traced his six pack with my fingers while I was by his side. I was as yet stunned he had one yet that made him significantly more
attractive.

We hushed up for 10 minutes and I had believed that Mason had fallen a rest as of now yet I surmise I was off-base. " A-A-Lissa, does this mean that you are my girlfriend and I win the bet? He exhaled and asked. I grinned at the idea and said "OK." then gave him a light kiss on the lips once more. After returning to silence, he handed me his phone, and I examined it. He was tweeting.

Concerning his current relationship status, he twitched. I saw all of the comments below. They were all about people praising us, some of whom criticized me, but I didn't care. I also noticed that his new bbm name was "Alissa+Mason." When I looked at Mason, I could see that he was happy now. He appeared to have just won 1 million dollars. He responded, "Love you more babe!" after I had just kissed him goodnight and said, "Love you Mason." Then I nodded off in his warm hug. Dreaming about .... well that is confidential.

CHAPTER NINE

SLUT ALERT!

At the point when he saw me he had a go at conversing with me however I disregarded him. He gotten my hand and pulled me back to him. He held his hands over me ensuring that I was unable to escape. My back was looked against his chest, and I could feel his relaxing. Gradually rising then, at that point, dropping down quick. He took an inhale and afterward started to speak "Alissa, kindly pay attention to me." I breathed out boisterously ensuring he heard.

"Fine you have 5 minutes miscreant." I said sounding somewhat irritated.

"Alright. What you saw back there isn't what it resembles. We weren't kissing, or possibly I wasn't. Mason made sense of. "Haha. Don't even think about it lie to me. I saw what I saw. You previously lost my trust think don't as well I will accept you so speedy. Additionally you just left me there at the house toward the beginning of today. I needed to take the transport, and you know how I'm with that thought. In the event that you truly focused on me, you would of came back yet you didn't!" I half hollered at him. "I could at absolutely no point ever connect with that skank in the future. You're the only one for me, "No doubt." She came dependent upon me and constrained herself onto me. I attempted to drive her away yet she was simply to tenacious. Additionally I left since I was upset. You didn't let me know you Liam actually talked. I returned, however you weren't there." Mason expressed anywhere close to out of relax. "Screw YOU" Furthermore, YOUR Skank. 5 MINUTES

IS UP SO BYEE." I hollered then utilized all the strength I had in me and pulled away. I strolled to my first period class. At the point when I arrived, everybody was checking me out. I genuinely didn't need the consideration I was getting. Rapidly I strolled to my seat and sat down. Then something peculiar occurred. Some person who I perceived as Keith locked the entryway and everybody pivoted to confront me. Goodness however, kid I. Whats occurring? They all addressed me and made sense of what has been going on with me in the first part of the day. Some young lady who I used to be aware said "Alissa that whore was all up on your person today. He truly attempted to drive her away however at that point she kissed him. He retaliated and pushed her to the ground however she got back up and stuck to him."

Next Jason and his young men what my identity was truly near spoke "Tune in Alissa simply take him back. That skank was the person who kissed him and he attempted to move her away. You realize me well so you realize I don't lie with regards to Mason. After both my young ladies; Emily and Lissa told me exactly the same thing as well. Everybody really said that he didn't kiss her back and she constrained herself onto him. I surmise I was off-base. I got up out of my seat and strolled to the entryway.

At the point when I was going to turn the handle Mason showed up before me. I got him by the neck and pulled him nearer to me then, at that point, crashed my lips onto his. At first he didn't answer however at that point soon later he did. His arm folded itself over my abdomen. I pushed him to the wall then, at that point, played with his hair. He nibbled my lower lip and I conceded him access. He slid his tongue into my mouth and delicate sliced it all over the place. I additionally did likewise to him. Behind the scenes you can hear the folks and young ladies rooting for us. I then pulled back and investigated his eyes when I expressed out of relax "I-I'm heartbroken, take me back please?" He grinned and lifted me up off the ground and spun me around. I was chuckling. I hit his back daintily while shouting for him to put me down. Minutes after the fact the educator strolled in and made a sound as if to speak. We froze and gazed toward him. "If it's not too much trouble, sit down class is going to start." He said in his stringent educator voice. We tuned in and took are seats. After when the class was done me and Mason left the homeroom connected at the hip. I was so blissful. My state of mind moved when I saw .....

CHAPTER TEN

THE FIGHT

I was so cheerful yet my state of mind moved when I saw Macy ... the skank from earlier today advance toward Mason. She took hold of him making me tumble all the way down. It was so amusing seeing her attempt what's more, get into his jeans, while he was looking sickened. He checked out me and argued for help. I grinned and sat idle. Then, at that point, she attempted to kiss him. I was frantic at this point. I got up and removed her from him. She fell to the ground and gazed toward me like she needed to tear my guts in half. She got up and did the most un-anticipated. I felt the sharp torment on my cheek as her hand slammed into it. Mason was behind me so he was ready to get me before I hit the ground. He looked so distraught at this point.

Alongside the horde of individuals encompassing us. They needed to kill Macy for how she just treated me. I got back up on my feet and said "Hello hun. I'm not the princess so don't think I wont keep down." I hit her upside the head and i'm almost certain I heard a break. She remained on the ground crying holding her nose. "y-you broke my nose!" she hollered. "I just helped you out, quit being a little bitch and be thankful." I murmured in her ear. She pulled my hair. "Alright listen little fucker. No one in this century pulls hair still. They battle and obviously you cant do that. So i'll tell you the best way to punch somebody out in the event that you don't relinquish my hair at the present time!" I expressed gazing at her hard in the eyes. She jumped in any case, let go. I left when I heard her shout bitch. I grinned furthermore, turned around and said aww gratitude for the commendation. As you may realize bitches are canines, canines bark, bark is from trees, trees are separated of nature, so you just called me lovely :) Her mouth was totally open however before she could say anything a few young ladies punched her also, took her out. I giggled and returned to Mason. He checked out at me one final time furthermore, told her that assuming she at any point lays one hand on me again he will tear her to pieces. I was blissful now I kissed Mason and afterward we headed outside to the parking area.

CHAPTER ELEVEN

Two Days More To Go

"Dear Grade 12 understudy. You have gotten a solicitation to the prom that will be held for yourself as well as your different schoolmates this week Friday. It will be held in the exercise center. Everybody is invited. Welcome... what's more, bring a date :)" As I read that little note over I could barely handle it. The school year had completed so quick in a flicker of the eye. I was energized at this point miserable. I would miss every one of my companions, and I don't know whats going to occur among Mason and me. I set the note back in my pocket and trusted that class will start. Prom was just 2 days away I actually hadn't selected a dress or inquired Mason.

I assumed he'd ask me anyway I have no idea why. Without regard to anything else, we must match if we are to actually work together. Quickly returning to the entranceway against the hard block wall, the educator arrived. I jumped and emerged from my positions. He was drenched in water when he walked into the study hall. He didn't appear to be particularly content, which was not a good sign. "You'll be writing your final assignment in class today. It will be about why students should respect their teachers!" Nobody held back as they groaned. Nobody was required to spend the last few days writing an article. However, we removed our PCs a few minutes after the fact the class was quiet.

Keyboard clicks were all you could hear. Then a little started to type. "Okay, so students should respect teachers because they are more experienced than we are and will teach us a lot in the future. The information provided will not only benefit us in the future but will also increase our job readiness." I took a moment to reflect, but the instructors' talking irritated me at that point. He had such a piercing voice that there were times when I wanted to sever his vocal chords. I proceeded with the article. "Screw this crap. Who thinks often about this exposition .... its fuckin dumb! Sure certain we ought to regard are educators sorry if we don't really. The end. By Alissa Martine. I grinned at my self like I just won a gold decoration. Alex was siting adjacent to me and he saw me grinning so he took a gander at my paper and when he completed the process of perusing it he burst out into giggling.

The instructor turned upward and began to stroll to are seats. I immediately eradicated the last piece of my exposition before he could see it. At the point when he strolled back to his seat, I took a gander at Alex and made a LOOOL face. We did a low high five then, at that point, composed. A couple minutes after the fact the chime rang and all you could hear were understudies supporting their opportunity. I left the homeroom and saw Mason hanging tight for me at the storage spaces. I approached him and kissed him on the lips then pulled back. "I missed you child." I murmured in his ear. "I missed you as well!" Mason murmured back into my ear making me shudder. We strolled inseparably to concentrate on lobby and afterward when we arrived we plunked down on the love seat. The educator wasn't here so that implied There's really nothing that that we can't do. Rather than concentrating on we followed through with something else. I wound my arms up to Mason's neck and pulled him closer. He crashed his lips onto mine and I kissed him back. Before long I felt his hand slither up my shirt and to my boobs. He delicately crushed it making me groan against his lips. I pulled back and expressed "None of that here child, perhaps after school." He glared yet put me down. He looked so miserable so I concluded that since the educator wasn't anyplace here we could have some good times. I moved my hand all the way down to his dick and abruptly he got invigorated.

"Hey, what are you up to? I thought you said no in school." I snickered and murmured in a sweet voice, "Gee, maybe just a lil bit is OK." He smiled and slid me onto his lap. I moved my hand until it was inside his jeans and then into his fighter. I looked at him, and he was having a good time with it. At that point, I gently crushed his dick, and he groaned. "It's not that loud. Try not to irritate anyone." I said it quietly. I drew my hand back as well, and soon found Mason riding me.

On top of me, he was While returning my shirt with his hand, he held my hands above my head. Click. My bra tie slid off, and I heard it. He inched his way up my top and then stopped at my boobs. He sucked on them, and I had to scream in retaliation. I couldn't help myself. I let out a loud moan, and he scowled. Then he started to pull away. "Hey, why don't we skip the rest of the school day and go to my house?" he wondered. That was fine with me because I had that idiotic instructor again. We gathered our belongings and went to the parking garage. I climbed into the car, and he soon followed. We went to his house and talked about the most ridiculous things. I got out of the car as soon as we arrived and dashed to the front door. I opened it using the spare key. Mason handed me over and walked into his room.

I paused, and shortly after, he joined me up there. I walked up to him and helped him get onto the bed. I said, "Recompense," and then I took his shirt off. I threw it to the ground before lowering myself to his areolas. I engaged my tongue, slid it around in a circle, and then gently sucked on them. I smiled while he moaned. Then he turned us over, placing himself on top of me. He took both my shirt and my pants off, leaving me only wearing what I was wearing. He looked at my body for a moment before licking his lips. After removing my bra and underwear, he lost his mind.

We were fanned out on the bed like star fishes breathing heavily 30 minutes later. "That was the best sex I'd ever had," he said. I agreed with him as well. Then, at that point, he asked me something

I had been waiting to hear for a week. "Alissa, will you accompany me to prom?" I got to my feet and hugged him. "Indeed! Good gracious, what took you so long to ask?" I responded. "I was so preoccupied that I completely forgot." I chuckled and eventually came to a halt. We were in his room, and there was an odd silence. I rolled over and examined him. He was at the time of rest.

He appeared to be resting quietly. Like a divine messenger. I pulled out my phone and took a picture. His eyes widened and he questioned as to what I was doing. Nothing, I said. He then took my phone from my hands and flushed when he saw my backdrop. "Take that off right now," he insisted. "Nah. It appeals to me." It was the photograph I had just taken. He marked the phone and returned it to me. "Aww, baby," he said as he drew me close and folded his arm over my abdomen, while I put my head on his chest. He embraced me tightly. It felt warm and loving. I giggled to myself, and we both nodded off minutes later.

CHAPTER TWELVE

GETTING SET

Emily, Lissa, and I were at one of the best dress stores in town. Because prom was only tomorrow, we didn't have time to look for the perfect gown. We looked everywhere but found no karma. That's when I realized I'd found the perfect dress for me. It was white and about two creeps above my knee. There was only one lash, which was cut into half circles that spread out from each side. The dress seemed to wrap around my body. It made all of the great elements stand out. There were globules scattered across the edge that were designed to look like a heart. It was absolutely fantastic. I found a pair of matching heels. They were silver and about 4 creeps above the ground. Dabs were also scattered across the front of the heels. So it was a perfect fit for the dress. I went into the fitting room and tried it out. I emerged from the fitting room a few minutes later. The young ladies simply looked at me with reverence. At that point, they must have liked it.

"You look amazing, Lissa," Emily said. She then gave me a few hoops and some jewelry that coordinated."Awesome!" Lissa read aloud. I smiled and walked back into the changing room. I removed the dress and replaced it on the holder. At that point, I re-dressed myself in my other clothes. When I got out, I noticed that both Emily and Lissa had chosen their dresses. Emily wore a baby blue dress. It was a long journey to the cold earth. Because there were no lashes, it was magnetized to her body. It highlighted all of her valid points and gave her a few fake breasts. (Not that i'm attempting to be mean) In the dress there was a cut so her right leg was completely uncovered. This dress would so make Alex slobber. Lissa's dress was red. It was just about as short as mine. The back was completely uncovered however with lashes. At the edge of the dress there were minimal brilliant globules. It was a strapless dress as well. The dress streamed down to her knee in an odd style. Yet at the same time it was decent. At the point when we as a whole were done dress shopping, we paid at the clerk. My dress approached $250, Emily's was $235 while Lissa was $232.45

At the point when we got done with paying we left to the parking area and got into my vehicle. It was a bit Mercedes. I adored this vehicle with for my entire life. Everybody was locked in and the packs where currently in the vehicle. I turned over the motor and pulled out of the parking area. "So where do you all need to go to eat?" I inquired. "Susan's kitchen. Recollect were meeting the young men there."Emily answered. I turned the radio on and are melody came on; Only A Fantasy - Nelly We chimed in with it and when the melody was done we were there. As you might realize I'm a quick driver yet i'm protected. I stopped in the main accessible space open the moved out the vehicle. The young ladies followed and we entered Susan's Kitchen. I saw Alex, Taylor, and Mason talking and finding a seat at one table so I skirted dependent upon them. I was behind Mason now. I put a finger to my lip asking the folks to stay silent. Then, at that point, I twisted his head in reverse and kissed him on the lips. He grinned against mine and maneuvered me onto his lap without breaking the kiss. Then, at that point, I pulled back and said "Heey missed me?". "All the more then you know" Mason answered with and kissed my lips once more. I grinned then the server came around and asked us what we would like.

We settled on a cheddar pizza. At the point when it came we as a whole dove in. The were no cuts left since we as a whole ate two. The server then came back with are drinks. I was sucking on a mint and gave one to him. The server was taking a gander at me now checkin' me out. eww I thought. I mean he was OK looking however I had him. He saw what he did so he pulled me near him and crashed his lips onto mine. I answered not missing a second. At the point when the server saw this his face dropped to a scowl and he left. "Haha your so amusing Mason" I said. He actually held me defensively. "I love you child." He murmured in my ear making me shudder in amuse. He sneered and afterward pulled away.

Mason and I were in his vehicle an hour later. He was taking me home, while Emily was taking Taylor and Lissa was with Alex. "Can I see the dress you bought for prom?" Mason inquired casually. "No way, it's a surprise. In any case, you must wear a white tie." "So it's white?" he wondered. "You can bet it's white. There is no more data "I said. He recently agreed with a smile. When we arrived at my house, I almost forgot the dresses were in my vehicle, which was with Emily. I called her and told her to arrive early and bring the dresses. She was alright with it. Before I left the vehicle I pulled Mason to me and kissed him. He kissed me back the I opened the entryway and got out and shut it. I was resting on the entryway and said "Love you, be at my home by 8PM tomorrow" he gestured and said "Love you as well, and goodness I can't have any desire to see my provocative darling." I become flushed and strolled to the entryway.

At the point when I was on the patio O said farewell to him as he drove off. I opened the entryway and strolled in. Mother was in the kitchen chatting on the telephone with a portion of her clients while father was a rest on the sofa. "I'm home." I said nonchalantly conversing with nobody. "Welcome home darling, suppers in the kitchen if your ravenous" Mother said however I recently gestured and approached my room. I was so worn out following a day of dress hunting. I fell on my bed and pondered how tomorrow would turn out.

CHAPTER THIRTEEN

PROM

It was 6:30 p.m., and Emily and Lissa were both at my house. I can't believe this evening is prom! It was only 1 hour and 30 minutes until Mason arrived. The young ladies and I had taken our dresses from the vehicle and were now sitting on my bed. I went to the storeroom and got three clear cotton towels, giving two to Emily and one to Lissa. Then we left the room and each chose one of the three restrooms in my house to wash up in.

Alissa

I ventured into my restroom and tried to lock the entryway. At the point when it was lock I peeled my garments off and got them from the ground and tossed them into the hamper. Then I strolled over to the

stand-up shower and turned the tap the entire way to warm. I didn't feel like taking a hot or cold shower. Simply a warm one would accomplish for this evening. At the point when it was at the right temperature I got in. The water felt so warm like how you feel when you first wake up on a cold winter night; Alleviating and unwinding. The perfectly clear fluid sprang out of the silver fixture and streamed down to my body. Come around drop. Skimming down my body then down to the channel. I snatched the cleanser and hurried everything over my body ensuring that I didn't miss a spot. Then I washed it clean. Next I got the shaving cream and spread it onto my legs. I took the shaver and slid it from down to up ensuring that all the hair was totally gone. At the point when I was done I switch the tap off and left the shower. I gotten my towel and folded it over my body and afterward out to my room where I began to prepare.

Emily

I strolled as far as possible down the stairs to the next restroom. This one was painted a child blue variety that matched the glass entryway for the stand up shower. I strolled over to it and turned the tap on to hot. Then I pulled my shirt off from my head and afterward slid my pants off. I picked them up and collapsed them into a slick heap and left them on the counter. The temperature was awesome so I got in. I let the water simply rush down my body in a quick speed then down into the channel. Then, at that point, I snatched the cleanser from its holder and scoured it onto my body. I put it back and got the cleanser and crushed a piece out and rubbed my scalp. At the point when it turned frothy I cleaned it out alongside the cleanser trails still on my body. It required around 3 minutes. For another minute I just let them water keep on running down my body then I switched the tap off. I remained in just a little then pulled the entryway open. The towel was right adjacent to me on the edge so I prattled it and wrapped it around my body then I snatched another and folded it over my head. At the point when I escaped the shower a virus spout of air traveled to me making me shudder. What was that? I got my garments and strolled as far as possible up to Alissa's room.

Lissa

I got the other higher up washroom. Thank god since I didn't feel like strolling as far as possible ground floor. Rather Emily got that one and i'm certain she was alright with it. I turned the handle and flicked the light change to on. Then I strolled in and shut the entryway behind me ensuring that I pressed the button on the entryway down to lock it. At the point when it was lock I peeled my garments off and strolled to the stand up shower. I turned the tap to warm. As a matter of fact it was more virus then, at that point, warm. Yet, I was alright with that however so I strolled in. I snatched the cleanser that was on the ground inside an emerald holder and slid it over my body then, at that point, I twisted down and set it back. I washed the cleanser follows away then took the face cleaning agent and scoured it onto my face. A couple minutes has passed and I washed it off in light of the fact that that was what the item guidelines said. "Stand by 3 minutes, then flush". At the point when I completed that I switched the tap off and snatched my towel which was hung up on the glass entryway. I got my self dry then, at that point, left the shower. My garments were still on the ground so I got them furthermore, threw them behind me. Then, at that point, I left the restroom furthermore, back to Alissa's room.

Emily and Lissa had recently completed the process of showering and presently they were in my room. We as a whole gotten are dresses and started to change into them. Mine embraced my body, while Emily's and Lissa's dress streamed. I needed to concede we as a whole looked fabo (Breathtaking) in are dresses. I strolled to my little work area in the corner and got out my make up; some eye shadow and lip gleam. Emily had recently decided to wear eyeshadow with a smidgen of mascara and Lissa had decided to wear a spot of eyeshadow with some blush. We applied are make up to are countenances and when we were done they looked professionnellement fait et magnifique pourrais-je ajouter! (expertly finished and exquisite might I add). Next for are hair we as a whole pick a similar style; straight. I took out my three irons and connected them. We fixed our hair when they became hot enough. It took about 25 minutes for everyone to finish. However, I must thank the accessory. I spotted it on the bed, strolled over to it, and snatched it. Emily wore it for me. Everything was now finished. We had our hair done, make-up done twice, and dresses on three times. I walked down the stairs with my heels in my hands, and the two of them did the same. We sat in the lounge chair, flipping through channels until we heard that distinct sound. 'Ding Dong!'

I quickly got up and opened the entryway. There stood three attractive looking men. However, i remembered them. It was Mason, Tyler, and Alex. I considered the young ladies and they all came into the front. "You look lovely Alissa, and both of you women as well." Mason said and given me a wrist band with roses connected to it. (Sorry I failed to remember what it was classified) "You look attractive that I wasn't even ready to remember you from the get go." I told Mason. He grinned and pulled me closer and kissed me on the lips delicately. "Snap" I turned and saw that Emily had the camera in her grasp and she just snapped a photo of us kissing. I become flushed and concealed my face into Mason's chest. "Alright, now is the right time to go women the limos hanging tight for us." Alex said and then left with Lissa close by soon Emily and Tyler followed. I could hear him murmur to her in her ear saying "You look exquisite angel." She grinned and embraced him. After I left the house with Mason and locked the entryway. We opened the silver handle of the limo and got in. It was just a 15 minutes drive cause the school was near here. At the point when we got out we seen that the school was finished and looked pleasant. At the top held a pennant that said "PROM" in cursive letters then there were decorations along the edge various tones. Everybody had separated and were presently conversing with the educators and different colleagues. Me and Mason strolled in and saw couples moving, while some remaining there needing to return home. He snatched me and maneuvered me onto the dance floor. A sluggish melody begun to play. I folded my arms over his neck and he held my midsection with his hands. I took cues from him. one two one two. He then pulled me closer and I rested my head onto his shoulder. "Alissa." Mason said. "Definitely?" I answered. "I love you." He said. I investigated his eyes and could see the adoration that was held in them. "I love you as well." I grinned. He then accomplished something I won't ever anticipate. He took out a little white box and got on his knee. He opened it and said "I love you Alissa Martine, and need to use whatever might remain of my existence with you. I vow to give you all my affection and consistently stay close by. Will you marry me?" I was stunned. The group had gone calm then you could hear them shouting saying "SAY YES! SAY YES!" I got onto my knee also, said "YES." I folded my arms over his neck and kissed him energetically. Then he pulled me up and put the ring on my finger. I panted at its magnificence. It was an exceptionally lovely ring. It was silver and in the center there was a blue precious stone that radiated brilliantly in the light furthermore, encompassing it were minimal silver precious stones. It coordinated well with my eyes. I turned upward and saw Mason grinning at me with desire in his eyes. The group were cheering. They generally complimented us. I was pulled a side from Mason and the young ladies generally checked out at my ring in wonder while the folks pulled Mason away from me and props him. They then, at that point, drove us into the center of the dance floor and the DJ playedare melody. "Just A Kiss - Lady Antebellum", we moved to it what's more, when it was over Mason kissed me again yet this time it was a kiss loaded up with such countless various feelings; love, desire, one, and so forth. I could feel the sparkles emit inside me. I was really blissful and frantically enamored with Mason and nothing could at any point change that.

This is just beginning of LOVE. Because Love is a never ending process.

Printed by Libri Plureos GmbH in Hamburg, Germany